PETROSINELLA

PETROSINELLA

A NEAPOLITAN RAPUNZEL BY

Giambattista Basile

ADAPTED FROM THE

TRANSLATION BY

John Edward Taylor

WITH ILLUSTRATIONS BY

Diane Stanley

FREDERICK WARNE

NEW YORK   LONDON

Illustrations Copyright © 1981 by Diane Stanley
All rights reserved. No part of this book may be
reproduced or transmitted in any form or by any means
without permission in writing from the publisher, except
for brief quotes used in connection with reviews written
specifically for inclusion in a magazine or newspaper.
Frederick Warne & Co., Inc.
New York, New York
Library of Congress Cataloging in Publication Data
Main entry under title:
Petrosinella, a Neapolitan Rapunzel,
by Giambattista Basile.
Summary: In this version of Rapunzel, the heroine
breaks the enchantment put on her by the ogress who
keeps her prisoner with the aid of three acorns.
[1. Fairy tales. 2. Folklore—Italy] I. Basile,
Giovanni Battista, 1575 (ca.)-1632. Pentamerone.
Petrosinella. English. II. Taylor, John Edward,
printer, of London. III. Stanley, Diane.
PZ8.P444 398.2' 1' 0945 [E] 80-25840
Printed in the U.S.A. by Princeton Polychrome Press
Typography by Kathleen Westray

For
PETER,
a real prince
D.S.

ONCE UPON A TIME there lived a woman named Pascadozzia who was expecting her first child. As she was standing one day at a window which looked into the garden of her neighbor, an ogress, Pascadozzia saw a beautiful bed of parsley. Immediately she longed for some and her longing became so great that she felt faint. At last she could not resist any longer. Watching until the ogress went out, Pascadozzia descended to the garden and gathered a handful of parsley.

But when the ogress returned home and wanted parsley for her dinner, she discovered that some had been stolen from her garden. "I will catch this long-fingered thief!" she cried. "And I will make him repent, you may be sure. This thief will be an example to others, so that they will know it is better to eat at their own firesides than to put their spoons into other folk's pots."

Pascadozzia went again and again into the garden, until one morning the ogress met her and in a furious rage exclaimed, "I have finally caught you, thief! Do you pay the rent of this garden that you come so boldly to steal my sweet herbs? By my faith, I will punish you well."

Pascadozzia, frightened and ashamed, began to excuse herself, saying that the parsley had not been taken for greed. "The Devil put me up to it," she cried. "He told me that the child-to-be would be injured if I did not satisfy my longing."

"Words are but wind," answered the ogress. "I will not be fooled by such prattle. Furthermore, you will have put an end to your life's thread if you do not promise to give me the child that will be born, boy or girl, whichever it may be."

Poor Pascadozzia, to escape the danger she was in, swore to keep the promise and the ogress let her go unhurt.

꽃   When the time came, Pascadozzia gave birth to a little girl so beautiful that she was a joy to look upon. And in the baby's tiny fist was a sprig of parsley and her mother named her Petrosinella, which means parsley.

꽃   Day by day Petrosinella grew and when she was seven years old her mother sent her to school. Every time thereafter that Petrosinella left the house alone, she would meet the ogress and the old woman would say to her, "Tell your mother to remember her promise."

꽃   So often did Petrosinella recite this message to her mother that poor Pascadozzia, weary of hearing her promise repeated and tired of being afraid, finally said to the child, "If you should meet the old woman again and she reminds you of that hateful promise, answer her, 'Take it'."

❧ Petrosinella, who was too sweet-natured to be afraid, met the ogress again the next morning. When the ogress repeated her usual request, Petrosinella innocently answered as her mother had instructed. Immediately the ogress seized her by the hand and took her into the forest, which was so dark and frightening that few ever ventured there. And then the ogress made a tower by means of magic and put Petrosinella in it. The tower was without doors or stairs and had only one small window. Through this window the ogress came and went, using Petrosinella's hair, which she had caused to grow very long, as a ladder.

❧ Now it happened one day, years later, when the ogress had left the tower for some shopping, that Petrosinella put her head out the small window and let her hair hang free in the sun. At that moment a handsome young man passed by—a prince, traveling to his parents' kingdom on the other side of the forest. Glancing up at the tower he beheld two gleaming waves of hair surrounding a lovely face, a face that could enchant all hearts, and the prince fell desperately in love.

❧ With a thousand sighs the prince begged Petrosinella to speak with him and she, who had also fallen in love, said yes. Hours sped by as the two young people exchanged loving glances, promises, and soft words. Finally Petrosinella, who saw how late the hour had become, begged the prince to go before the ogress returned home.

❧ After such visits had continued for several days, Petrosinella and the prince vowed to meet in the tower chamber, but only in the evening, when the moon plays with the stars. So it was that the prince advised Petrosinella to give the ogress some poppy juice that night to make her sleep. This Petrosinella did and the ogress was soon soundly snoring.

❧ At the appointed hour the prince went to the tower and, at his signal, Petrosinella let her hair fall out the window. The prince climbed up and crept through the little window into the chamber. Soon the night became too short for their vows of love and plans for escape. The prince begged Petrosinella to come down with him on a ladder of rope, but for a reason she herself did not understand, Petrosinella refused.

❧ The next morning, before dawn, the prince descended by the golden ladder of Petrosinella's hair to go his way home.

❦ The young couple's meetings continued for many nights until one evening a gossipy friend of the ogress, who was forever prying into things that did not concern her, caught sight of the prince climbing into Petrosinella's window. The next day she visited the ogress and warned her to be watchful as Petrosinella was in love with a princely youth and she suspected they might be planning to run away together.

❦ The ogress thanked the gossip for the information and said that she would put a stop to the visits immediately. As to Petrosinella, she said, it was impossible for her to escape. The ogress had laid a spell upon her and this was it: unless Petrosinella took in hand the three acorns which were hidden on a rafter in the kitchen, she could never leave the tower.

❦ While they were talking together, Petrosinella, who was suspicious of the gossip, listened with ears wide open and overheard all that passed.

And when night darkened the forest and the prince came as usual (the ogress being fast asleep), Petrosinella asked him to climb to the kitchen rafters and find the acorns, knowing that they were the cause of her enchantment. He brought them down to Petrosinella and she slipped them into her pocket.

Then, having made a rope ladder, they both descended to the ground and ran away toward the prince's kingdom as fast as they could. But the gossip happened to be watching them, and she began to shout and make such a noise that the ogress woke up.

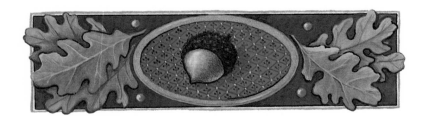

Realizing that Petrosinella had fled, the ogress descended the same rope ladder which the couple had fastened to the window. As soon as she reached the ground she set off after the lovers who, seeing her coming at their heels faster than a run-away horse, almost gave themselves up for lost.

But then Petrosinella, remembering the acorns, quickly threw one to the ground in desperation. And lo! instantly a large bulldog rose up, terrible to see, and with open jaws and furious barks it flew at the ogress, meaning to make a mouthful of her.

❧ But the old woman, who was more cunning and spiteful than the Devil, put her hand in her pocket, pulled out a loaf of bread, and threw it at the dog. Immediately the dog hung its tail, stopped barking, and fell to gobbling the bread. Then the ogress turned to chase the lovers once more, faster than ever.

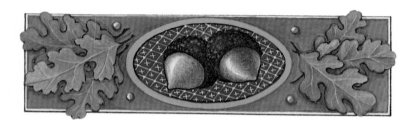

꽃 Petrosinella glanced behind, saw the ogress coming again, and threw the second acorn to the ground. And lo! a fierce lion, lashing the earth with its tail, rose up and, shaking its mane, opened its jaws nearly a yard apart.

The lion was ready to make a good meal of the ogress when she, looking desperately around, spotted a donkey's skin drying from a tree. Putting on the hide, she ran right at the lion who was so startled by the change from ogress to donkey that he bounded away as fast as he could.

Having survived this second challenge, the ogress, still dressed in the donkey skin for fear that the lion was following, turned again to pursue the poor lovers. Petrosinella, hearing the clatter of her heels and seeing the clouds of dust that rose up to the sky, realized that she was coming a third time.

In terror of their lives Petrosinella now threw down the third acorn before the swirling dust. Immediately a hideous wolf rose up and without giving the ogress time to play any new trick, it gobbled her up just as she was, still in the shape of a donkey.

So the lovers being now free from danger went their way at a slower pace to the prince's kingdom, where, with his parents' consent, the prince made Petrosinella his wife, and his princess.

And so, after such great suffering, they experienced the old truth that:

> One hour in port, the sailor freed from fears
> Forgets the tempests of a hundred years.